E
KR

Kroll, Steven

The candy witch

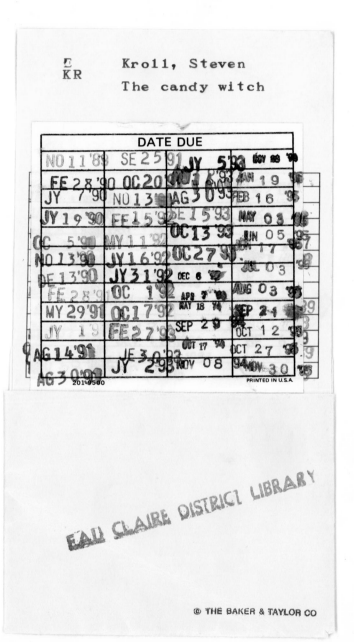

DATE DUE			
NO 11 '89	SE 25 '91	JY 5 '93	NOV 23 '90
FE 28 '90	OC 20	JUL 16 '93	JAN 19 '95
JY 7 '90	NO 13 '91	AG 30 '93	FEB 16 '95
JY 19 '90	FE 15 '92	DE 15 '93	MAY 03 '95
OC 5 '90	MY 11 '92	OC 13 '93	JUN 05 '95
NO 13 '90	JY 16 '92	OC 27 '90	JUN 17 '97
DE 13 '90	JY 31 '92	DEC 6	JUL 03 '95
FE 28 '91	OC 1 '92	APR 7 '93	AUG 03 '95
MY 29 '91	OC 17 '92	MAY 18 '94	SEP 21 '89
JY 1 '91	FE 27 '93	SEP 29 '95	OCT 12 '95
AG 14 '91	JE 30 '93	OCT 17 '94	OCT 27 '95
AG 30 '91	JY 29 '93	NOV 08 '94	NOV 30 '95

201-9500   PRINTED IN U.S.A.

© THE BAKER & TAYLOR CO

The Candy Witch

by Steven Kroll

illustrated by Marylin Hafner

Holiday House, New York

Library of Congress Cataloging in Publication Data
Kroll, Steven.
The candy witch.
SUMMARY: Because her good deeds are not noticed,
a small witch steals every trick-or-treat bag in
town on Halloween.
[1. Confectionery—Fiction. 2. Witches—Fiction.
3. Halloween—Fiction] I. Hafner, Marylin.
II. Title.
PZ7.K9225Can   [E]   79-10141
ISBN 0-8234-0359-9

For Emily, with Love...S.K.
In Loving Memory of Harvey...M.H.

Maggie the witch lived on a hill near the town of Chester. Everyone in her family liked to cast good spells for people.

Brother John changed pillows
into purring cats.

Mama Witch flew around
turning garbage
into fruit trees.

Papa Warlock liked
giving bald men hair.

Maggie liked sticking candy into people's pockets. She liked filling empty refrigerators with food. But no one in her family noticed the things she did, and sometimes, because she was so little, no one noticed her at all.

One night at dinner, Mama Witch said, "Maggie, when are you going to start doing good deeds like the rest of us?"

"I *do* do good deeds," said Maggie. "You just don't pay attention."

"What a thing to say," said Papa Warlock. "Why, of course we pay attention."

But that night, when Maggie made David Jennings' flowers bloom, no one noticed.

Her mother was singing in the shower,
her father was busy mixing a potion,
and her brother was reading a book of magic.

"Nuts!" said Maggie. "If no one
notices when I do something good,
I'll have to try something else!"

She waited until the morning of Halloween. Then she flew to Ellen Perkins' house and cast a spell. Ellen turned on the bathroom faucets, and lizards tumbled out everywhere.

Maggie flew to Patty Russell's house and
changed a dining room chair into a blueberry pie.
Patty sat down on the pie. Then her mother

found a frog in her pocket, and her father's hair turned curly. The coffee pot poured chocolate syrup, and Patty fell over a cow on her way to the school bus.

Maggie followed the bus. When she got to school, she sat on the roof, thinking of more mischief.

When Diane got up to answer a question, her books fell on the floor.

When Myron came to bat during recess, an orange fell out of his ear.

When Eric opened his lunch box,
it was full of mice.

    "Something weird is going on in this town,"
said Eric.
    And everyone agreed, especially Bill, whose milk
had just turned into a flower.

Maggie went home.
Her father was busy
mixing another potion,

her mother was singing
in the garden,
and her brother was reading
a book about outer space.

"Oh, rats," said Maggie. "Nothing's changed."
Then she had an idea for that night.

As it began to get dark, the children gathered in groups to go trick-or-treating. They were dressed as skeletons, cowboys, gypsies, witches, and pirates. And as they went from house to house, the candy in their trick-or-treat bags grew heavier and heavier.

By the time the children got home, their bags were almost too heavy to carry.

Sharon Ripley was lugging hers
up the stairs when it disappeared.

Her brother Philip was putting
his under the bed
when *it* disappeared.

Patty Russell was showing
her candy to her mother
when, suddenly, it was gone.

David Jennings had just spilled his
all over the floor. As he went to
pick it up, it turned into air.

The next morning at school, everyone was
talking about the missing trick-or-treat bags. Not
a single child in town still had one. Ellen Perkins
was angry. David Jennings and some of his
friends were crying.

On the roof of the principal's house next door, Maggie sat with all the candy. One hundred and seventy-three trick-or-treat bags.

But then she noticed David Jennings crying in the school yard. And Diane Hollander. And Sammy Bow.

Maggie began to cry too. Her sobs grew louder and louder.

Suddenly Mama Witch, Papa Warlock, and
Brother John appeared.

"What's the matter?" asked Mama Witch.

"Oh, Mama," said Maggie. "I wanted to make
you notice me. And instead I've made the children
unhappy."

Papa Warlock took her in his arms, and Maggie told the story of her day's mischief and the missing trick-or-treat bags. When she was through, Papa Warlock and Mama Witch and Brother John kissed her and said they were sorry.

"And we'll try and do better in the future," said Papa Warlock.

"But what can we do for the children?" asked Brother John.

Maggie smiled. "I know," she said.

As the children got ready to leave school that afternoon, there was a lot of noise in the yard. A large sign was stuck on the lawn. The sign said: COME TO THE CANDY FESTIVAL! RIGHT NOW! TOWN SQUARE! MAGGIE THE WITCH.

"Now we know who stole the trick-or-treat bags!" said Ellen Perkins.

The children all raced off to the town square.
The fountains were spouting lemonade. They were
overflowing with Hershey's kisses, candy apples,
M&M's, peppermints, caramels, jelly beans, and
lemon drops.

Over on the town hall roof, Papa Warlock said, "What a terrific party, Maggie."

And Mama Witch added, "The fudge was awfully good."

Brother John would have said something too, but he had eaten a lot of caramels and was fast asleep.

Maggie flew over him and cast one more spell. When Brother John woke up, he'd find candy in his pockets.